A MIDSUMMER'S ENIGMA

Girts Vitelis

Michael Terence
Publishing

First published in paperback by
Michael Terence Publishing in 2019
http://mtp.agency

ISBN 9781913289454

Thanks to a special person this has become a reality, so thank you, my fellow Scorpio, for making sure I didn't quit this journey, you've seen this all the way through now.

Of course, big thanks and huge hugs to my family who were a big part of this journey too…

I was walking down this dark eerie path that leads to the huge cathedral up on the mountain top. The trees swayed in the midsummer's breeze and the weird shapes all around were the result of the full moon shining down with its silver bright light. On this path to the cathedral an ol' owl was sitting on a tree branch. "Whooo! Whooo! Whooo!" was what interrupted the deafening silence of the forest around. The big blue eyes of the owl offered hope, when I glanced at them, hope in reaching the cathedral safe and sound.

I've been talking about a cathedral and I haven't even described it. It's my first time going there so all this is how local villagers have described it and what they've told me about it. The cathedral was only done building five years ago, 1864 to be exact. I've been told that it is very grotesque and intimidating in its appearance. It stands tall over the mountain top with its high towers. The light reflects off the colourful glass panes and plays tricks on village folk. It's made from stone and every tower has a gargoyle just below it. Crows and ravens are the only birds seen to be attracted by the gargoyles. It took a while to get it all done, with all the strange occurrences that tend to happen there.

People in the village believe the cathedral has been built on sacred burial grounds. The villagers that went there would go missing. Some would return after days and seemed not themselves anymore. Their manner of speech had changed, their stature, their happiness seemed to have gone its own way. They wouldn't eat nor drink anything. Some might say that they had been possessed or their souls had simply left them.

Children have been warned to not wander off to the cathedral. Three kids have gone missing since the cathedral has been built. The whole village spent days upon days looking for them to no avail. One kid had been found hanging from a tree… and what looked like he had been there for some time. Even dogs don't go anywhere near that cathedral, they must sense that something isn't right there. No flowers grow on the mountain top either and the trees are all leafless, just plain old branches hanging over, waiting to break off and rot into the ground.

As I finally reach the mountain top, a dismaying sight struck my eyes. The breeze that was on the path, is nowhere to be felt. No owls either, just a couple of old crows looking angrily at me. A complete silence once I scare the crows away. A silence more deafening than the forest below.

Even the most calm and peaceful of minds would have trouble being just that here. Such a dark and empty feeling. No wonder people are scared of this place.

My heart starts racing faster, beating heavily. "Du dum! Du dum! Du dum!" My eyes and ears become very alert, even though there is no one here but me and the ominous silence. My mind tells me there is no one here but my intuition tells me otherwise. I get this feeling that someone is behind me… watching me… waiting for my next move…

I approach the cathedral with great caution, wary of my surroundings. Anything or anyone could jump out at any moment. My heart already is racing uncontrollably. A scare like that and I'll be gone with the wind.

Why would I want to come here you may wonder?

The stories the villagers have told me intrigued me very much. The children that went missing and the way people return completely different… I have a feeling that I will find some answers here or at least clues that will point me in the right direction. I'm petrified to go and investigate but I won't get my mind at peace if I don't try and figure this out and maybe the families that are hurt will finally know what happened and be at rest… if I don't go missing or anything bad happens to me. I can't let myself cloud my mind with thoughts like these, got to go on and investigate, for my sake and for other's sake… to find answers.

I walk towards the huge oak doors of the cathedral. I grab the gargoyle face knobs and with all my might I open the heavy doors. That smell that drowns my nostrils… filthy rotten smell. As I take my first step, three rats run out in front of me. They stopped and glanced at me. Those blood-red eyes looking at me as if I was food to them. I grabbed a stick and scared them away… no rats are eating me today.

Anyways, endlessly tall ceilings are fascinating inside. There are so many arches connecting the columns. It hasn't been cleaned up for years now, but the work put in is mesmerizing and all still in good condition. Nothing seems to be falling apart or hanging down, waiting to be ripped off. I'm surprised at how it hasn't been ruined from top to bottom. My guess is that some sort of a supernatural force is protecting it. Keeping it from complete destruction. It must be the sacred burial grounds at work here. When I asked around the village if anyone knows anything more about the burial grounds, other than them being there, they all shrugged their shoulders. No one knows for sure, just rumours and whatever someone chooses to believe. What the village elders said was that the grounds had been there before the first records of the village were taken. The village has been there for more than 200 years now so they must be really old or even ancient burial grounds. It would be good to find out more about the origins of the burial grounds or even to know who or what is buried there.

The village is located a few hundred yards from the lush and dense forest at the base of the mountain. It's not the biggest nor the most beautiful of villages but the people here try to be as happy as they can be. The King, however, has different ideas and is always on the backs of the villagers, always needing more money and rations from them and not caring that most of them have families that need to be fed. Already asking from the villagers a quarter of rations he is now demanding they give him three-quarters of everything they produce and grow. The winters tend to be quite tough these days and everyone working hard in the village needs as much as they can produce. And sometimes whatever they have planted doesn't grow if the drought has hit so that just makes everything harder for everyone.

All these little houses have been built generation upon generation. Most of them are these little wooden boxes, each with their own flower garden at the front and a little chimney on the rooftop, puffing out smoke from a fireplace on which a pot of soup is boiling. The lovely smell of the soup spreads throughout the village. Should've brought some food with me as I'm getting kind of hungry.

The children are running around and jumping up and down and enjoying their time off work as much as they can before they have to go back and help their parents. They are singing folk songs and the laughter of the children echoes throughout the village and can be heard at the forest. Everything is livelier with kids around. Two words, joy and happiness.

Now there is always someone who has to keep a close eye on the kids as to protect them from wandering off to the cathedral. Curiosity is what got the three missing and wandering off without letting anyone know always leads to trouble.

There is one thing I haven't figured out yet, what might be that supernatural force surrounding the cathedral? Ghosts maybe, demons or something much worse? This is what is keeping me up these past few days. After hearing all that the villagers had to say, after doing some sketching, I still haven't arrived at any conclusions. Hopefully, me exploring this cathedral now, will provide some answers.

I have reached the end of the huge hall, the podium where the bishop used to read out his prayers. Oh the prayers… what if the bishop wasn't praying to the God, for the God but for something evil? Bringing some kind of damnation into this world from the deepest depths of Hell. The sinners and the deadly would walk the Earth and bring ruin upon everyone.

On the podium, there is the Holy Book and three candles. The Holy Book is big enough and has these red covers and a black cross on the front cover. As I flick through the pages, I come across a passage that is missing, few pages ripped out. Can't quite figure out what was on them. But it seems I have found my first clue. All I have to do now is to figure out where it might lead me to, what dark secrets I may stumble upon and if I'm truly ready to uncover this mystery.

The writing has faded quite a bit throughout since the book is hundreds of years old. The few words I can make out read as such:

"Vendetta… will… strike… upon… thee."

"The… Abomination… shall… rise."

"Time… is… of… the… essence."

Just these three sentences. And it doesn't sound like anything good either.

'Knock, knock, knock!!!" Huh? What was that? Who was knocking there? Is someone there? Is there really someone other than me here or is all this getting to me and my mind is playing some kind of tricks on me?

I want to go and investigate where the knocks came from but I don't think that it's a good idea. My heart started to race fast again. If it keeps this up, I won't last that much longer. My hands started to shiver and my knees too. It suddenly got a lot colder, freezingly cold. A cold feeling covers my body. I take a deep breath to calm myself before going. I have to find out what it was. As I take a step, I feel a hand on my shoulder… I look back, with a fearful face, unwantingly… nothing there. And it's not cold anymore either. Now I'm really scared. Whatever it was, it did a good job of making sure I was terrified. My body is still shaking. I can't even think properly. All I've got on my mind is the knocking and the hand that I felt on my shoulder.

I already haven't slept in a few days and this will for sure keep me up for a week straight. Good thing I've brought my flask with some brandy in it. That will make me calm down and keep my mind off this so that I can focus on finding the clues to solve all the mysteries that surround the cathedral and the villagers.

I find it very impressive how the villagers are able to get on with their lives as well as they have, after all that has happened. It's always tough to lose someone but to lose a child that has yet to grow up and have their own family is unbearable for parents. I don't have kids of my own yet so I can only imagine what it's like for them. The villagers did tell me that the parents of the child that was found hanging from the tree, were not allowed to see him. That grim of a sight it must've been. And to go outside and see the grave of their child… that's not something that I would want to see. No parent should ever see their child go. I've explored all of the village but haven't gone around to the graves of the children and don't plan on doing so.

Going back to how the King is treating the villagers, he's always been like that towards them. He's very young for a King, only has been around thirteen summers. He's got a lot to learn and has people teaching him and showing him the correct ways. But it turns out that he's very stubborn so that only complicates things, especially to how he treats people that are lesser than him. Nothing that the common folk hate more than a King who treats them like garbage, is greedy and un-respectful. No one even knows exactly how he became the King. Some say he poisoned his father, others that he smothered him in his sleep and some even say he stabbed him with a dagger. His father was a good King. Treated everyone equally and was good to the common folk and by doing so was respected by everyone.

I open the back door of the cathedral it has a cemetery behind it. It's not too big and has been there for many centuries but no new people are buried there, since everyone is afraid to even set a foot on that mountain top let alone go to the cemetery. The bigger the tombstone the wealthier the person was. Moss has grown over on almost all of them but three have been left untouched by it. And what's more interesting is that the names have faded on these three tombstones. The more I explore this place the more questions arise. Questions that I can't seem to find the answers to.

I came here from London. I read about this village and the strange occurrences they have experienced in the newspapers. I was very intrigued and me being an inspector I felt it was of utmost importance for me to come out here and explore and find and provide answers. The midlands always have had a record of strange and weird thing going on here but this, by far, is the strangest of them all. My job in London would provide I see many weird things but not like this, not supernatural.

I had to leave, my beautiful wife to be Estamond, alone in London. 'T was a decision very hard to make. She understood that it's something I have to do, to be able to help others and maybe in doing so prevent future incidents that have struck the villagers. Not a day goes by that I wouldn't think about her. Writing letters to her is what I look forward to at the end of every week. Something that relaxes me and keeps my mind off things. I just don't know for how long I'm staying here in the village, definitely not leaving here until I solve the mysteries and find all the answers.

As I was looking at the tombstones a breeze picked up. Leaves that lied dormant suddenly picked up and blocked the warm sunlight from reaching me. It only lasted a moment and felt very strange. I looked at those leaves and followed with my eyes to where the wind was going to take them… nowhere, they just picked up and fell back down after that moment. What I saw next was even stranger. On the three tombstones that aren't covered in moss, blood-red leaves covered them now. I don't think this is meant to be normal. So, I walked over and I picked up those leaves. I could make out what looked like some kind of pattern on them, like veins on a human body but it was the colour of it that was weird, black. Dark like the deepest caves and the deepest woods. I've no idea what to make of this. Some would say they're just leaves and there's nothing weird about them but nothing around here is normal and after what I experienced earlier I get even more of a notion someone or something is after me, giving me clues that I don't know where they will take me. The more I delve into this the more I feel it'll be harder to get out.

Oh, there is one more strange thing about this village and that what surrounds it. The mountain has an intricate cave system. No one has explored it fully. No one has the necessary courage to do so. A place shrouded in darkness so terrifying that rarely anyone would dare to enter those caves. Those who haven't returned. But the weird thing is, the village folk all say that they hear strange noises at night coming from the mountain. Sometimes people crying, sometimes people screaming and sometimes children laughing.

They say those strange noises last only a little while and they have noticed that they happen three nights only, the night before full moon, during and the night after the full moon. I didn't hear any such noises on my way to the cathedral even though it's the full moon. Maybe on my way back but I rather choose not to hear them. I already have experienced enough weird, supernatural things. The last thing I need is for my ears to hear and for my mind to want me to go and investigate.

I've now gone through the cemetery and have reached the well down by the little stream. Though there isn't much of a stream now there. It's grown over with tall grass and you can hear the crickets play their nocturnal songs. The silence isn't as dull with their songs playing and keeps my mind open and focused. There is an old redwood bench by the well that's rotten in places with rusted legs and the handles too. An indication it's been here for quite some time.

The well is all dried out as I lean over and try to see how much water is there. I do see something as I shine the lantern light inside but it's something I least expected and to find in a well… I see a hand… reaching out from the mud that it's stuck into. I need to get closer to be able to tell if it's a child's hand or a grown-ups. But from up here, it looks like a child's hand. From what I can tell it doesn't look like it's been there for too long. I don't want to believe this. It can't be. Not another family that has to go through the pain, the sorrow, the suffering. Everyone seemed to have gotten back to their old ways and they were happy. And I don't think I am able to tell this to anyone, let alone the parents, if this is a child. But before I let these thoughts cloud my mind, I have to get down there and uncover the body. I have to wait until daylight and I have to go back to the village to get a rope to be able to get down this well.

"Huh? Very strange as suddenly I don't hear any more of the cricket songs…"

Now a complete silence and darkness has surrounded this little corner by the well. Not even a little breeze, just feels like the time has stopped in place. The clouds have covered the moonlight. And the light seems to be running out in my lantern. It won't last me long enough to walk through the cathedral. Thanks to the little light that I have left, I see a few dark shadows fly over my head but my eyes can't make out what they were. This grim feeling covers my body and I get shivers down my whole body. I hope there won't be another hand on my shoulder feeling…

Every morning when I wake up back in London, as I look out through the window all that I see are the grey clouds that shroud the London skies. The air is heavy to breathe in and smelling, all the waste from the factories going up in the air and slowly killing everyone. I do wish that Estamond would've come with me to this village. The air is all fresh and the havoc of the city life is nowhere to be seen or heard or even felt. A complete freedom and the surrounding beauty of the nature right at our fingertips. But I couldn't have her experience all this, the strange and the weird that has affected the village folk. She already isn't happy that I work as an inspector in London. I know she constantly worries about me but at the same time she is happy that I help other people and not just myself. One of the village elders, Alder, he thanked me when I first came here to the village. He thinks, he's sure that I'll be able to uncover all the mysteries that are present here. He's been around sixty-seven winters and is the oldest of all the village folk and the wisest of them all. He looks over the village together with two other elders, Eder and Gaius, fifty-six and fifty-eight winters respectively. They all work together to keep the village in place and everyone safe to the best of their ability. One of the kids that went missing was Gaius's grandson. He would stay out the longest and look for him to no avail. He still goes out and looks for him every night and doesn't give up his hopes of finding him.

I once took Estamond to a circus in London. It was meant to be ***"a spectacular and an unforgettable memory"***. That's what the leaflet said. One of the worst decisions I ever made was going to this 'show'. The way they treat animals and how they use those whiplashes to hurt the poor creatures of nature. The elephants kept their heads down, incapable of looking up and standing properly because of all the bruises and rashes that they had. And I remember from reading in a book that elephants are supposed to have tusks but their ones were missing and I don't even want to know for what they were used. It was all so heart-braking. We walked out of it the instant we saw them use a whiplash. Everyone else in that tent seemed to be enjoying themselves and laughing at the poor creatures.

Why am I talking about a circus, you may ask? Well, it's because of the feeling that I felt the minute we walked out of the tent. I had this feeling that someone was behind me, watching me and then a hand on my shoulder… the same exact feeling I felt here once I entered the cathedral. Only now I remembered because it felt familiar, very familiar and very strange.

I just hope that I will manage to get back to the village to get a rope and return during daylight to go down the well. The light is running out every minute. A few more shadows I see fly over my head. Are those bats or birds? Can't hear a sound either. The silence is so dull that I might be seeing things that are really not there. I start running. I don't know where just know that I have to get away from here before the light completely goes out and before I completely lose my mind. This place has already managed to cloud my judgement so many times. I run past the cemetery. Think I saw a figure standing by one of the tombstones. I just have to keep on running, the light is almost gone. I'm starting to hear things as I hear a 'swoosh' one after the other. With each 'swoosh' that I hear I feel something touch my hair. I've got shivers all over my body and I'm starting to lose my breath. I'm almost at the hallway. What I hear are the sounds of things flying past me and braking against walls and the floor. As I approach the giant doors they suddenly shut close in front of me. I was running so fast that I couldn't stop in time and ran into them.

Huh!? Where am I? What happened to me? What is this place? These are the questions that run through my mind as I wake up. I have no idea what is going on or what happened. The last thing I remember was me running from something and then it becomes dark, nothing. I look around and all I see is a room, a candle on a table in the middle of the room and a chair in front of me. Can't move my hands as they're tied behind the chair. I feel dizzy and confused, don't have a clue what is going on.

There seems to be no doors noir a window in this room. That smell though, like rotten meat, drowns me. The floor has bloodstains all over. Some big pools of blood were there. Scratches can be seen in the floor, deep and what I believe are broken off chips of fingernails. The walls are covered with bloody handprints and long streaks of blood on all of them. This all feels scary and I feel that something bad is going to happen. I'm very certain now that I was on to something. Someone was following me and tied me to this chair. I wonder, what do they want from me? I have no answers to give them, all I have are questions.

Can't tell night from day in this place. Don't hear anything of any importance either, just what I think are branches scratching off against the outside. In one of the corners of the room, three rats seem to be chewing on something. I see something shiny there, between all the rotten flesh.

Wait, is that my ring? As I look at my hand… my finger has been cut off. I don't feel a thing, so it must've been done a while ago. The ring was a gift from Estamond. It has an engraving ***"My life is complete with You by my side"***. It means the world to me. I have to get it before the rats eat it. Got to find something that I can use to free myself. I looked and looked across the room and nothing. I end up breaking the chair as it was the only thing that I could think of. The noise was loud and scared the rats away and I was able to safely take the ring. I hung it in the chain that I'm wearing so it won't get lost now. Now I have to figure a way out of this dreadful and nightmarish place.

I took a closer look at those scratches on the floor. Someone was trying to open a hatch before being dragged away. I forgot that my finger was cut off and so as I pull upwards it started bleeding a lot. I had to make a bandage from the sleeve of my shirt to stop the bleeding. The hatch I did manage to open. Slowly and steady I cautiously walk down the stairs. There lit torches on the walls and the water reaches up to my ankles. The only sounds I hear are those that rats all around me are making. That devilish stare that they all possess, so evil and intimidating. I grab a stick I found in the water and head on towards the light. Nothing much to see here as I walk through one passage after another. These tunnels are like a maze so I just picked a direction and walked. I did start to get dizzy again, must've lost a lot of blood. My vision started to become blurry too. I have to keep on walking, have to find a way out…

So this is the village that Galen came to. It is very nice here. And so quiet and peaceful. Complete freedom from all the city havoc. And the fresh air and the breeze blowing through my hair. I'm not even worried that the wind will ruin my hair. All these kids running around full of joy and happiness. All the worries in the world do not exist in their minds. Only freedom… *magnifico*[1].

I hope Galen will be happy to see me here. I kept it a secret and wanted to surprise him. He's always put everyone else above him and has helped when he can. So, I was happy that he doesn't care only about himself. From the letters that he wrote to me, it seems that there are a lot of strange things going on here. Things he can't even explain. Strange occurrences and kids going missing. But what I fear the most is what he said in the most recent letter that I have about something or someone following him, watching him… *terrificato*[2].

"Ooh, what is that lovely smell?" is the first thought that I have as I walk through the village. Lovely flowers everywhere and the scent that they have… tansies, geraniums, summer heathers and

---

[1] Magnificent. (Italian)

[2] Scary.

Chinese primroses and some small pine trees too… *magnifico*. It's a nice change of scenery after all the dark and greyness that London provides. And this isn't even all, I've still to go down to the forest but I already can't wait to hear all the different bird sounds and see the wild animals and flowers and of course, smell them… *magnifico*.

I wonder, when is Galen is gonna be back? And no one here can tell me that either. They say he's been gone for three days now. Ahh… what if something has happened to him? No, no, no got to believe he's alright and that I'll see him very soon. He's just caught up deep investigating and exploring I'm sure. I would like to go to the cathedral up on the mountain-top but the village folk are saying that I shouldn't, that no one should go there. But I am going to the forest and no one can do anything about it… *finito*[3]. I want to see an owl there, those big blue eyes that they have See deer and squirrels and listen to the bird songs and eat some wild berries too, mmm… *delizioso*[4].

[3] The end; over and done.

[4] Delicious.

My vision isn't as blurry now but I am still feeling dizzy. Can't stand this smell, you never get used to it. As I pass every corner in these tunnels, I see more and more filth and rotten insides. Something has been busy. There isn't much for me here to investigate so I just carry on to find an exit. Just so many turns and tunnels. Like a whole new world down here, unexplored and untouched. As I walk through these tunnels, I see drawings on the walls and I feel that I have to inspect these. The drawings are depicting rituals, sacrifice rituals and ones that I can't quite make out what they are. The sacrifice rituals would explain the filth around here. I'm pretty sure the drawings are depicting summoning rituals too so that would explain the supernatural that has struck the village and what surrounds the cathedral. I remember the sentences I made out from the book and I wonder if I can connect those to some of the drawings. The one about 'Abomination' is one of the summoning rituals, I'm sure. I can make out letters just above the drawings but I don't know if they're in the right order; "F… I… R… U… C… E… L". I've got no time for this so I just take a note of them.

As I take another turn, I see a bright light ahead of me. I have to see what's there. This is a room very similar to the one I was in only difference being that it has a door which obviously is locked. But someone was here as they have left their lanterns.

"Boom... BOOM... BOOM!!!" Huh? What was that explosion? Where did it come from? I have to get back to the village. It's going to be quite hard to run in this dress though... *fretta*[5], *fretta*. I can see a lot of black smoke coming not too far from the train station. I hope that no one is hurt, especially kids. I was gonna leave my medical kit at home but I thought it might come in handy but I never wanted for there to be an accident and explosions involved. I've got to hurry, I can hear screams. Everyone, mothers, fathers, kids together with loud cries. I just hope I can get there in time. As I get closer and closer, I start to smell the smoke. Everything so grey ahead of me I can barely see where I'm going. I left my medical kit where Galen was staying and it's a bit of a walk from the train station so gotta run faster. As I run past where the accident happened, my God what a grim sight it was. All those people... all the blood and the distraught... *terrificato*.

That's strange, why is the door open? I'm sure that Galen wouldn't have left it open. As I walk in, it's all just a mess everywhere, like someone was

[5] Hurry.

looking for something. Clothes all over the floor, drawers broken, even the flowerpots have been all broken. What were they looking for I wonder? What has Galen gotten himself into? Least my medical kit was left untouched. Now I have to rush back to the accident.

What was that loud noise? Sounded like an explosion. Must've been because the tunnels have caved in behind me. So, there's no way of going back the way I came and the only door in this room is locked too. From one trouble straight into the other. I have got to find something to open the door with. One after the other I take rocks from the cave in, each bigger than the next so I can maybe, knock the door down. It seems to be working as cracks appear and I can see through but what I see is nothing good. There are some ten big bags hanging down from the ceiling. Blood is dripping and the whole floor is just covered in pools of it. In a corner, there is a table and on it there are dozens of tools and all covered with blood. All this is making me terrified as I don't know what to think anymore. What I thought before to be supernatural might really be something else. People, some really bad people if they're capable of doing this. I need to get out of here and get back to the village. I still have to find out who that was in that well. And I've got to deal with all this. I'm not telling others of this yet anyways. Maybe when I'll know more.

- Help! Help me!! - shouted Eder. I can't move my legs!

- I'll be with you in a second - I replied.

There are people lying around everywhere who all need my help. It's a good thing that others came as well and help as best and as much as they can. I haven't counted yet, but it looks as if there might be anywhere from ten to twenty people dead and another twenty injured or seriously hurt. Nothing left of the train either. Those explosions caused many people to sustain damage from the flying pieces. Without proper treatment, these folks might not last much longer. Many need amputations which only complicates things as I don't have near enough resources to perform operations on such a scale. There are a few kids dead too. Only more sorrow for the village after this accident. Is this bad luck? Someone punishing the villagers maybe? If so, then what for? These are nice, kind and lovely folk. One after the other this village is struck with misfortune. But still they find enough to be as happy as they can and show great kindness towards others, as they showed it to Galen and me… *bellissimo*[6].

[6] Very beautiful.

Where am I? What is this place? How did I get here? I must've fallen asleep. I don't remember ever being here before. What am I doing in this abandoned tunnel? And there seems to have been a cave-in or something, it's blocked off. What is that room over there? Hello… anyone there? The door has been smashed open with something. Oh my!!! … so much blood… everywhere… and those body bags hanging from the ceiling… what the hell is going on here?!? I have to get out of this place. Can't stand the smell of it all and the blood… think I'm going to be sick. That table in the corner, maybe there's something that I can use to open this door here in the room. Ahhh… all bloody and covered in guts… someone has a serious problem in their heads. This drawer here… maybe there's something there… Eureka! A key. This must be a spare key, only a dumb person would leave it here. And now to get out of this torture chamber. But what about all those body bags up there? I'm just going to have to come back and get them down later. Huh?? What's that noise coming from the other side of the door? People talking?!? I can't let them see me… I'm going to have to hide in the corner where they keep the body bags…

- Now, son, you're going to learn how to do this properly. 'Cause you don't want a repeat of the last time do you now? -father told his son.

- Yes, papa, I promise I'll do it properly this time - the son replied. - Papa, but who is that guy that you caught and tied to the chair?

- I don't know son. Was walking down the tunnel and saw him trying to open the door.

- But why'd you have to tie him to a chair? Could've just hung him like the rest of these bastards.

- I had a feeling he might come in handy, help us out provide us with information.

- What information? How to hang people? Hahaha…

- Haha… very funny. No you *idjet*[7]. To tell us everything he saw at that cathedral and what clues he found. I was at the cemetery when I saw him running from something…

- What do you think it was that he was running from?

- I've no idea but it seemed as if he was terrified.

[7] A variation of the word idiot.

- Oohh… scary. Ok, so how you do this properly again?

- You take that big cleaver that's on the table, sharpen it up before you use it. You're gonna start off by cutting off the rest of his fingers, then the limbs and then finally the head. Then carve out the heart and feed it to the dogs. Then you will put them in the body bag, the limbs and what's left of him, I'll hang it up and then we'll come back tomorrow to finish the ritual.

- Ok, papa… Papa?!? I think you better come and have a look at this…

- What is it now? Do you not know how to use a cleaver anymore?!?!? Ohh…

- I thought you tied him up to a chair, papa? What are we gonna do now? He's probably long gone now.

- Then what are you still doing here? Run after him you idjet, there's only one way back so quit yapin' and start runnin'!!! I'll catch up with you.

I remember this one time when I went on a journey to the new land, India. It was a while back, before I met Estamond. Just jumped on a boat and sailed across the seas. Sunshine, rain and more rain struck us nearly every night. Waves banging off the side of the ship and rolling over the side. Almost half of the food we had brought with us was destroyed by the sea. Rats had infested the ship and ate our bread and meat. Hunger had struck us.

Lucky for us we saw this small island in the distance and the captain decided to change the course towards the island. From afar seemed as if there were plenty of trees there to provide us shelter and we bet our lives that there was plenty food there too. The beach was so beautiful, the sand so warm, a warmth that none of us had felt since we set sail and it felt so good between our toes. The lush trees, filled with bananas and coconuts and further inland pineapples, were growing in this huge field. And the sight of those flowers… the greatest painters ever would find it hard to recapture this sight on a canvas.

This honestly felt like the paradise we all dream of going to when we'd die… am I dead? Is this all real? It can't be as I could never have imagined I'd get to see and be in such a beautiful place. I don't even want to go back ever again. This island has everything we need to survive. On the other side of the island there is this lagoon, crystal clear water… all the starfish and corals can be perfectly seen. Pick a colour, any colour and you'll find it in there. And the dolphins jumping up and down through the waves and singing their songs, their little babies by their sides trying to keep up with the grownups… this place really is peace on Earth.

So, those two are the ones who have killed all those people… and for some sort of a ritual. What for though? And I still don't know what I'm doing here. I know they said that they brought me here to question but it still doesn't answer my question, what am I doing here? The last thing I remember is that I was in London getting ready to go to a village in the midlands and investigate strange occurrences there… wait, so maybe this is the village and I have wandered somewhere while investigating? What has happened to me? I think it is amnesia or something… First things first, I need to find my way back out of this place. How am I going to do that now? Those two have left now so I can try and make my way out of this place. I should follow them. Maybe by retracing my steps, I can get back my memory of where I've been and what I've seen since arriving here. I hope that I've encountered people here as they could surely help me. Still, I wonder if I managed to find out what was going on in the village. What was causing all those strange things? The village folk disappearing? Oh it seems as I don't have my notebook with me. I hope I left it in the place that I was staying in… which, of course, I don't know where it is now… I write down everything in it and do sketches as well, my notebook will surely help me get my memory back. Finally, sunshine. Ok… so it seems as though I was in a cave. This is one cave that I don't want to return to… definitely.

I seem to have wandered quite far on the island as I don't see any of my shipmates. I'm going to have to look for them and set up a campfire for the night. I've been told that nights can get quite cold in places like these. Luckily there are plenty fallen down trees that we can use for the campfire. Good thing we brought the axe with us too. But before I go and look for them, I need to make a torch, can barely see anything in this forest. The skies are full of stars and I think I can make out a few constellations too… Ursa Major… Ursa Minor… and that must be Draco… and that is Cassiopeia. There are more of them but I was never an astrologist so I can only name these. I wonder what's inside this cave here… maybe treasure?

Ohh my… can't call that treasure. Skeletons… and a good few of them. I wonder though for how long they've been here? And they all seem to have fallen asleep and never woke up. A peaceful death is what many of us want… I don't know for how long we're going to be here for on this island but I sure do feel like spending an eternity here. But where are the rest of the guys? They seem to have disappeared into thin air…

But seriously, where have they gone now? The island surely can't be that huge. And it's almost sunrise. The strange thing is though, I haven't encountered any animals here yet… well apart from the dolphins in the sea. I hear birds chirping and singing their songs but I don't see any. But the sunrise… oh what a beautiful sight that is. The island lighting up with colours, the shadows making all these weird shapes on the soft sand and the lush green grass inland. And finally, I see the birds as they fly above my head as the sun rises over the horizon. But these are birds I've never seen before… with beautiful colourful feathers. A smaller one, a baby I'm guessing, landed near me and wants a piece of my banana. –Here you go little birdy. But please don't bite my fingers off ok? The birdy loves the banana. I'm naming you Grey because your eyes are grey. I'd love to have one of these birds, Grey in particular, but with me travelling now it wouldn't be a good idea. I'm just going to have to sketch you in my notebook Grey.

Alder, do you think we should tell that young lad Galen what we know of the burial grounds beneath the cathedral?

- What's the point now Eder? He'll ask why we didn't tell him anything before he went there. Better leave it as is.

- But you do know he hasn't been back in a few days now?

- Yes, of course, I know. And what do you want me to do about it?

- Well, we could go and look for him…

- And not return ourselves. Is that really what you want? You know what happens to people who wander there.

- But it happens because you let them go there. You've never told anyone the truth about those burial grounds.

- People don't need to know the truth… They are not ready for it.

- And what if he returns… with answers and this mystery solved? What will you do then? Kill him? Lock him up? Hang him?

- Maybe. And who is to say he will return at all? You know what lurks around those parts…

- No, I don't know… I don't want to talk about it… you know I don't.

- Then stop acting like that. He won't find out anything… I've made sure of that.

- What if his lover, Estamond was it, goes after him? What will you do then? Don't think that even you would allow her to die.

- I've taken care of that too. There's no need to worry. I've arranged and planned everything so that no one would ever know or find out what is going on here or what has already happened…

- No… don't tell me you've hired them again… why? You know what they did the last time they were here…

- That got a little out of hand…

- You call that 'a little'? You saw that kid hanging from that tree. How could you let them do that?

- I didn't know they were going to do that. I only told them to scare the villagers so that they wouldn't ever dare to go to the cathedral and interrupt our work there. You know how important it is to us, to the village.

- No, I don't know. I only know that what you tell me… which isn't a lot, may I remind you.

- You know that what you need to know. If you knew more that would only raise questions and you know how I get when people question my actions. Everything I do I do for the good of this village.

- I know I know. I guess I just want you to be less ruthless with your actions is all I'm saying. They've all been through enough suffering and don't need any more of it.

I wish that I could tell Galen all about my past… I haven't told anyone about it. I know he wouldn't say anything, only that he understands why I did what I did. I just can't get myself to tell him… *mi vergogno*[8]. I was learning to become a doctor and my family was going through some very, very… difficile… tough times. I couldn't let my little sisters and brothers live on the street so for a little while I was working at a brothel… No one knew and lucky for me, no one ever told my family that either. I'd have the higher-ranking clients and so they paid much, much more than they usually do. In three days I'd get as much as a farmer earns in a month selling their produce at a market. Quickly enough I was able to help my family solve all the problems and forget that we were ever in a situation like that.

I moved away, changed my name and eventually met Galen. And I never looked back at what I had done to get to where I am now. But every now and then I feel that I should tell Galen about that time I spent there. Just thinking about it again makes me upset. It all left me broken both emotionally

[8] I'm ashamed. (from Italian)

and physically most of the time, the only time it didn't was when I did manage to fall asleep and have a good night's sleep, which rarely happened. It definitely is something I won't ever do again… *decisamente*[9].

Having lived that lifestyle, it provided different perspectives on what the nightlife is actually like in the city, how people live on the streets, illness plaguing the majority of them. I was working at a brothel for a little while, it wasn't the best noir the cleanest but for so many people, they live in such bad conditions for years and some even their whole lives and they have no choice about it. They are willing enough to have whatever 'home' they can get as to not be on the streets in the cold and the wet. And the way how people would try and stay away from these people… all thinking that they are better than them only because they've got a job and are educated. During the night time, there'd rarely be people who'd walk through those parts.

That's actually how I met Galen. I had already moved away and started over. This one night I was walking through one of the impoverished parts of the town and this man runs right into me, knocked

---

[9] Definitely.

me and all my books on the ground. He helped me up, we both looked deep into each other's eyes… he introduced himself and offered to walk me home. So, we talked and talked and talked… what felt like *la eternita*[10]. I didn't want this to end, it was something I had never experienced before. He had to go to work early so he asked me if I'd like for him to come around tomorrow and we could go on a walk and to the beach as well. Of course, I couldn't say no to that. I love long walks and I love the beach it's… *magnifico.*

[10] Eternity.

Hmm… what are the two of them talking about? Something about "not telling people the truth" and "hiring some people"? Then that about "a kid hanging from a tree"? Seriously, what the hell is going on here?! Nothing makes sense and what do I even do now? Where do I go? This path here… I wonder where it will lead me to. This dark forest surrounding it is giving me a bad feeling. It looks even spookier than the tunnels in that cave. And that owl sitting in that tree… creepy looking owl. That deafening silence, so dull, so intimidating. It's like an otherworldly force pulling you towards it, irresistible. So, I do follow the path, mostly in my search to find answers and get my memory back. It is very strange though. The whole time I've been on this path the only other alive being I saw was the owl. No other birds singing their songs or animals suddenly running on to the path from the woods… dead woods. This path is leading me to the mountain top. I saw that cathedral there when I got out of that cave. Strangely, as it may seem, I'm starting to have this familiar feeling the closer I get to it. Like I've already walked on this path. Now I'll definitely get my memory back, if not all then hopefully some of it. Oh… a *nice* change of scenery… some crows are looking at me angrily. The trees all around this cathedral look even spookier than they did on the path. The cathedral isn't any more welcoming. Those tall towers with all the gargoyles, their big mouths, claws, and the very sharp looking teeth… I know that they are made out of stone but it certainly doesn't feel that way. Feels like they were alive a long time ago and then were somehow frozen in stone. As I open the giant oak doors of the cathedral, I can see the sun coming up and revealing a dreadful sight inside…

I thought I'd find the two of you here. We are going to have a serious conversation.

- Alder?! About what?

- I just saw Galen come through a cave. I thought I made it clear that the two of you need to keep him tied up and get all the information out of him.

- See papa, I told you that we need to use chains.

- I know son. Mr Alder, can you please give us more time? I promise you that we'll get him!

- You had your opportunity. How am I supposed to know that the two of you won't screw up again? I can't afford any screw-ups. People will start asking questions soon.

- What you want us to do then?

- I want you to set up a trap for him. A torture trap because I want to see him suffer and get every last bit of information out of his mouth.

- Ok… but what we will do about her?

- Leave her to me. I've got something special planned for her… Just make sure that no one sees you and you do it all at night time.

- Do you want us to torture him just enough that he's barely alive or that the torture kills him?

- Barely alive and then I'll kill him myself.

- Ok, but you are gonna have to give us anything that we'll ask for. If you want it the way you want it, that is.

- I'll provide you with anything you need. Just don't screw up this time.

- Papa! This looks like a good spot to set up the trap. It's in a dungeon and I haven't seen any of the village folk come near this place.

- Good. Now we just need all the tools. But remember what Alder said?

- Which part?

- He said that we've got to do this during the night.

- Wasn't that the torture part?

- We'll do the whole thing in the night. The less light, the fewer eyes.

- Papa, what do you think Alder is going to do to her?

- I don't know. But it did sound like he has something serious planned for her.

- I'm kind of starting to not like what we've been involved in. I don't want for innocent people to die.

- What's with you? Not too long ago you were ready to torture the poor bastard!

- I don't know. I just see the way that Alder talks about them and it feels like he's just crazy, lost his mind.

- Well, there isn't much that we can do but listen to his orders. After all, he's been grateful to us.

- But what about the other two, Eder and Gaius? What if they reveal to everyone what Alder has been doing? Everyone will be after us too because I doubt that Alder will stay quiet.

- In that case, we've got to make sure that Alder doesn't speak of us. We build this trap and then go after Alder. End all of this.

- But maybe in that case we go and get the other two elder's support? Have them help us take down Alder.

- Son, that just might be the best idea you've had in a long time.

- Thanks. Think we need a plan now. Set things to do.

- Well, first we build the trap, lead him here, trap him and go away for a while. Let things play out themselves. In the meantime, we get the support of Eder and Gaius. Then we all go after Alder.

- Sounds good to me. The faster we do this the better. This dungeon is giving me a bad feeling.

- I agree. I'm getting a bad feeling too. I'm very certain that many people have died in this dungeon… too many people.

- The faster we get out of here the better.

I have a fond memory of the time when I was in Egypt. The second we stepped off the ship in Cairo, I took off my shoes and socks and enjoyed the warmth of the sand in the morning sun. The ruffle was very different from that in London. Every person, that I gazed upon while walking through the bazaar, was enjoying themselves. Camels, funny looking animals, but I've been told that they are like horses to us, provide a helping hand… or should I say "*hooves*". Cats are running around everywhere. Cats are sacred animals to the Egyptians. A person who hurts one will receive a serious punishment. The people are friendly too. I don't know if that's because they know I'm a traveller and that I have money but I don't care about that anyways. I came here to explore, see new places and animals and enjoy whatever Egypt has to offer. The heat is getting hotter by the minute here. I can't even begin to imagine what the heat is like in the desert. The first place I want to travel to now, is down the river Nile. I've heard stories that there are behemoths. They are these extremely large and powerful beasts that roam the wild there, destroying everything that comes across. When they open their mouths, a grown man would be able to walk right into them. Truly mythological beasts. People tell terrifying tales about them. Tales of how they attack people and eat them alive with one bite. But they're just tales to me, I want to see them for myself. I want to see all the different species of animals that Egypt has to offer. I want to see them as I simply do not know when or if ever I'll come here again. As we travel further down the river, a huge herd of animals has gathered around to quench their thirst in this blazing heat.

As I open the giant doors the dreadful scene reveals Eder's body lying on the floor. No blood… so it wasn't that type of a murder. But upon investigating the body more I find that there are no rope marks or marks of any kind for that matter. Who would do such a thing? Was it those two who were chasing me before? On the first glance I don't see any clues either since there's so much on the floor, broken stuff and just a big mess everywhere. I do look closer though and I find muddy footprints. They're not Eder's as his boots are dry, the mud is all dried up clearly quite a while ago. That suggests he was here for quite some time. So, someone was following him… but how cold they have killed him without leaving a trace on the body? There's really nothing… no scratch marks to indicate a struggle… no foreign hair nor broken fingernails. What if I'm going about all this the wrong way, what if it's not a murder, an ordinary murder, revenge killing? What if I leave the *'normal'* behind? What if to solve all this I should trust my instincts, my gut feeling?

I do remember that I was reading in the newspapers, before coming here to the midlands, that these missing people cases seamed very unnatural. Three kids went missing and every newspaper in England wrote about that… **"Enter the forest… There is no return for You"** is what one of them wrote for their title. It is true, as other than the kids, adults never returned as well. But if this really is a case of the supernatural, how does one go about solving it?

With my memory gone… do I still carry on in this cathedral… in the search of getting it back or do I go back to the village, if I can find a path first of course, and get some help from the other two elders… and then come back here? Would make for a good opportunity to get to know everything they know about Eder, in order to solve his seemingly murderous case. I should get to know more about Alder and Gaius as well, as I left off quite quickly and didn't get a chance to get to know them better. They surely know way more about the village, its history, how it came to be, what and if there have been mysteries like these in the past.

That's settled then, I'm going back to the village. It's daylight now so I should be able to find my way back to it. What should I do with Eder's body? I won't leave it here, on the floor for the rats to chew on. I'll bring it here where the long benches are and cover it up with something, blankets hopefully… if I can find any that is. Wait… what is that under this picture frame? Eder's body was on top of it this whole time…

"*Ahh...*" I wake up screaming. These terrifying nightmares. I can't take this anymore. They're making my skin crawl. Me being a nurse, I'm used to seeing blood and all that comes with it. I shouldn't be like this. It all started after that terrible train catastrophe. I can barely sleep at all and when I do sleep all I have are these nightmares... *sono irrequieto*[11]. I thought that if I went back to visit that spot again, that maybe those nightmares would stop... I was wrong... Oh I was so wrong. As soon as I got there, all I could see was the colour red, the blood, the pain... could only hear the screams and the cries. It was so much that I fell to my knees e pianto[12]. The fact that I have been here for a while now and that I haven't seen Galen since I got here makes all this a lot worse.

I'm struggling to cope, can barely even focus. I've lost my appetite and spend the days just wandering around in this little house. I'm afraid to go outside as I can't tell the difference from reality or another nightmare. Oh my dear Galen, where have you

---

[11] I'm restless.

[12] And cried.

gone? You sure would know how to help me, even if just by being close to me. *Solitudine e paura*[13] are the only things I know now… that I'm capable of feeling right now. I wanted to get out of the everyday havoc that is London and make Galen happy to see me but it all has gone so horribly wrong. How do I get out of this jail that my mind is locked into? Do I pray? Do I beg for mercy? Or do I simply give in? It is very tempting but I don't want to end up like some *persona pazza*[14].

I want to have my own kids, see them grow up and have my grandkids. I want to move out of the city and live by the sea, grow old there and die in peace, feeling that I have achieved something and knowing that I'll leave this world, for the afterlife, with something to be proud of. So, I can't just simply give up like that, there's still so much I want to achieve… that I have to achieve. But all those people that died, they too had so much that they wanted to achieve and I couldn't save them. I know that I couldn't have saved them all but I still feel that I should've done more. Their trembling

---

[13] Loneliness and fear.

[14] A crazy person.

faces are all that I can see now… all that I'm able to see.

What was that strange noise? It seemed to have come from those bushes over there. The last thing I need now is for something else to happen. It's like some higher force is saying "There's more for you Galen". I was on my way back to the village but reluctantly, I will have a look at where that noise came from. It sounded like bangs, like someone banging on something. And to make matters even more peculiar what I found under Eder's body was my ring… the one that was a gift from Estamond. I've no idea what it was doing there or how it even got there. It's the one thing in the whole world that I wouldn't leave behind just like that. I *noticed* that I'm missing one of my fingers. So, I must've hung the ring in the chain that I'm wearing… Oh no, did I do **that** to Eder? Where would I even get the thought of murdering him? For what reason? I don't remember that he was hostile to me the first day I got here or anything like that, on the contrary, quite the opposite, he was kind and welcoming. Maybe he did something to me… or I to him? Maybe there was a struggle between us and it was all just an accident? It's all just an emptiness in my head, as I can't remember anything from the time I left the village for the cathedral and to the day when I realised that my memory is gone. I'll figure it out but first, I have to find out what was that strange noise. These bushes here, it's so hard to get through them, I need an axe or something. The bangs keep getting louder and louder, so I must be very close. Finally, I get through the bushes but all I see here is just grass… there's nothing here. I spent a good while here just walking around to see if I can find something here, anything really. Huh?! What was that? As I hear the bangs again, I felt vibrations go through my legs. Now that's a good hiding spot… or whatever it may be. There must be a hidden door of some sorts somewhere on the ground surely. Ha! I knew there had to be one. Right… do I really want to take a look? I am an inspector after all, so it's my duty. Jeez… it's so dark in here. The cave that I was in, you'd expect no light there but there were torches everywhere. So it's a surprise that there are none here, well from the first impressions that I have. I climb down the ladder and lucky for me I do see light in the distance. The hard part now is to get there in one piece. I just hope that there are no holes in the ground for me to fall into.

-Aaahhh!!!! Where am I?!? What is this place?!?

- Hush woman. You're wherever we've taken you.

- Papa, are you sure it's a good idea you let her talk?

- Sweet Jesus! Who are the two of you? Murderers or something?

- I said, hush woman! And yes son, there's some good information we can get out of her… I can guarantee it. Just go there and look out for him, he ain't far now I bet.

- Papa, where are your manners? You didn't introduce yourself… we didn't introduce ourselves to the lady. My name is Rodrick and my father's name is Ramon, we're pleased to meet you… though excuse the circumstances.

- And you don't need to introduce yourself… Estamond – Ramon added.

- Excuse me, but how do you know my name?

- That's… that's none of your business! – Rodrick shouted from the other side of the room.

- Ramon was it? Could you at least tell me what am I doing here and why am I strapped to this… this device? *Torturarmi*… to torture me? Is that what this is?

- To answer your questions, no and yes. No, 'cause you're in no position to be asking questions. And yes, you are in a torture device and as such, soon to be tortured.

- Why??? What good reason would you possibly have for torturing me?

- Well, we're a couple of people short. Once they arrive, everything will be made known to you.

- Was this your idea? Are you the instigator behind this ordeal?

- No, someone else gave the order. And it's someone you know…

- Who?! You've got to tell me!!!

- We've nothing to tell you. You'll find out everything in due time – said Rodrick.

- So just shush and lay there, we ain't gonna say more! – Ramon added.

- You can't tell me to shush. I can talk if I want to!

- But I don't want you to talk. I want you to stay quiet and wait for what's coming to you.

- Ramon, at least have the common courtesy to tell me as to what have I done to be tortured?

- It's not necessarily what you've done but what someone else has done, like I said, someone you know.

- Galen?!?!? *Non ci credo*[15]. What has he done? He only came here to investigate whatever has been going on in this village.

- He stuck his nose where he shouldn't have. We have orders, it's not like we hate the man or anything. If we don't follow our orders, much worse things will happen.

- And who's giving you those orders?

- Papa, I think we can tell her now. I can hear them coming.

- Can you see who's coming though?

I heard someone scream in there. It was a woman. What would a woman be doing in such a bad place as this? No one should be coming here, it's not a good place at all. So dark and damp and terrifying. I wonder though, who are the people in there? I can't just go and walk in there, with no idea whatsoever of what it is that I'd be walking in to. I need to take a little time in finding out more. But

[15] I don't believe it.

there might not be any time, the woman might be in trouble and all that I'd be doing would be 'taking a bit more time'. Are those footsteps that I hear? Is there some kind of a meeting going on here today? I get this familiar feeling though, a feeling that something like this has already happened. I better hide and let them pass, can't allow anyone to see me here now.

Maybe this is all a really bad dream, a nightmare? This just can't be real. I can't believe… I won't believe that Galen has done something, let alone something that would put me in danger. He doesn't even know that I'm here. And even if he had done something, the least they could do is allow for him to say his side of things. It's only fair and just. Alder, Eder and Gaius told me themselves that Galen had gone off to investigate. I don't want to believe that something has happened to him either but no one has seen him since, least no one has told me that they've seen him. They might be keeping that a secret from me too. More than anything, here, it is easier to think about what they are keeping a secret. Everything seems to be *avvolto nel mistero*[16].

[16] Shrouded in mystery.

- So, who is it that you see coming, son?

- It's Alder with Gaius. But I don't see Eder anywhere though papa.

- Huh, that's strange. I always thought they stuck together like a hand with a glove.

- Why are they coming here? – Estamond asked while quietly trying to get out of the straps.

- I thought I told you to stay quiet! – Ramon shouted, – They are the ones who we have been waiting for, but of course, we're still a couple of people short.

- Papa, what are you gonna say to Alder when he'll ask why **he** isn't in the torture device?

- Rodrick!!! Do you even realise that you just told her who's behind this?

- I'm sorry, I'm sorry. I didn't mean to. She'll know anyways so what's the point in hiding it anymore?

- You don't know. Maybe Alder had planned something 'special' for her.

- So what if she knows? Alder can still do whatever he had planned. What worries me more papa, is if he's gonna show or not.

- He has to. Everything that had happened was leading him here.

- So, you're finally admitting that this was all planned beforehand. – said Estamond, after managing to free her arms.

- There were plans but most of them changed as that's what plans do. The one that didn't change was the one where you got tied to that torture device. – Rodrick added.

- I only hope that you both, Alder and Gaius and Eder will suffer for what you are doing here you'll… *soffrire un dolore inimmaginabile*… you'll suffer unimaginable pain!!!

- I think what you were trying to say was that you are going to suffer unimaginable pain, not us. – Ramon said angrily, - and what language is that, that you mix in there?

- It's Italian. I wouldn't expect someone like you to even know where the Kingdom of Italy is.

- Sorry to disappoint you but we went to the Kingdom of Italy last year. – Rodrick said proudly.

- What would the two of you even be doing there… never mind, don't even bother to answer. You both are a disgrace to people, tying a lady to a torture device. Shame on you two.

Oh my beloved Estamond. You can't imagine how much I miss you, just the sight of you would lift my spirits as I'm becoming more and more exhausted with this investigation, deprived of my senses and the will to carry on. I've lost my memory of the days that I've been here and don't even know my next step to take. I do realise that something is going on here and that someone or something is trying to cover their actions. There's been so much killing and so much suffering here. I'm in this underground dungeon, hiding and listening, trying to make out what those people are talking about in the room. I'm waiting for the right moment to go in but I'm even starting to doubt that the right moment is going to come. I'm surprised that I haven't lost my mind yet… or maybe I have and all this is just me imagining and seeing things that I want to see… that my mind is making me see. The things that I do remember seeing just recently, they would make your skin crawl. And what's making all this even weirder is that I found Eder dead, mysteriously there was no indication of a struggle or anything, none at all.

Day hmmm… I've lost count now.

Galen.

-Silence!!! All of you! – Alder ordered as he walked in, - I don't want to hear a word out of any one's mouths!

- Mr Alder. It's good to see you again - Ramon said politely. - We've followed your order as you wanted except that we didn't trap him but lady Estamond.

- How dare you do this Alder! I thought you were a good man, one who looks out for his own. And I expected better from you Gaius. Could've at least tried to stop him. – Estamond said disappointingly.

- Ms Estamond, you can't possibly imagine for what reasons we are doing this, all of this. There is a certain order to things. And there are certain steps for one to take in order to prevent grave things from happening… and sometimes you just do such things to despise people - Alder replied while looking out if either Eder or Galen can be seen approaching.

- Mr Alder, I think we're gonna have to start the ritual without them - Ramon suggested.

- Gaius! You go over to the other side of the room and start setting up the altar! - Alder ordered Gaius as he took out this ancient-looking book.

- Consider it done Alder! - Gaius replied.

This book, it looks very, very old. I think I saw stitches all around it. I assume it's covered with human skin… and written in blood… *orribile*[17]. I wouldn't even dare to touch such a book, unholy and created at the cost of others, more of a curse than a book. While everyone was getting ready to start the ritual, Rodrick came over to me and whispered into my ear "I won't tell them you've undone your straps and I will help you escape this place." I didn't know what to make of this. 'Should I trust him or should I not?' I kept asking myself. After all, how could I, he and his father were the ones who took me down here, forcefully and strapped me to this device to **torture** me. But then again, he did seem a little off with this whole ordeal, like he was acting to fit in and to please his father. Well, Galen would say that I should 'follow my instincts', him being an investigator. So, I'm going to do that, he showed kindness, Rodrick, in a situation when no one else did, so I do trust that he will help me escape.

[17] Gruesome.

Oh my… As I open the door, what a grim sight it is right before my eyes. What is Estamond doing here? When did she even come to the village? Estamond, like she's some kind of sacrifice, strapped on a table. Alder and Gaius, they're here too, and those two that were chasing me.

- Someone owes me an explanation!!!

- Welcome Mr Galen, we've been waiting for you! -Alder said.

- Ah Mr Galen… Looks like you've finally found this place. – Ramon added.

- Alder, the two men that were chasing me, what's the meaning of all of this?

- Well, there is no pleasant way for me to put this but this is the place where you will meet the end of your journey.

- But why? What have I done that is so bad? I thought you wanted my help about the missing people? To find out the truth?

- And I'm quite surprised you got as far as you did. It's one of the reasons why you must meet your doom now… you got in too deep.

- People deserve to know. All those families. They were kids Alder, just kids…

- And they will know, they'll know whatever I decide to tell them.

- You heartless monster!!! – shouted Estamond.

- And monsters deserve to be put down.

- No Galen. The only people dying tonight will be you and your dear Estamond.

- What has she done to you?

- Nothing. I just want for you to suffer. The last thing that you will see will be her dying, the dark in her eyes as she fades away. Then and only then will it be your turn.

- We thought they were both gonna be sacrificed? Like the kids. – Ramon expressed his surprise.

- There is no sacrifice you fools. I used the two of you so you would do all the dirty work and kill anyone I tell you to.

- Were you a part of this too Gaius?

- Yes Galen, all five of us. We had no idea it was going to go this far. Alder told us sacrifices had to be made to keep the village safe. – Gaius replied.

- You all must have no hearts. How could you possibly allow anyone to do something to little kids? It's wrong, so very wrong.

- We don't have to explain ourselves to you, as no one's going to remember you after tonight. – Alder said with certainty.

- We'll see about that. I won't go down without a fight and I definitely won't let any one of you lay a finger on Estamond.

- I wouldn't be so sure. You are outnumbered here. Yes, we might be of age now but we still won't go down without a fight.

- If you say so…

- Ms Estamond?

- Y… yes… yes, Rodrick?

- You should come with me now. While they're all arguing, I'm gonna undo these straps here, set you free. They won't even notice.

- Why… why are you doing this?

- I don't want to see any more people killed, enough is enough. Should've stopped long ago.

- And after… after you release me? What then? You sure they won't notice?

- Look at them, they're in the heat of it all, arguing and making sure one is better than the other and that none of them has done anything bad. And after the escape, I'll make sure that you and Mr Galen get to safety and will be able to go home.

- But they will all be chasing after you, hunting you down like an… *come un animale.*[18]

- You mean like an animal? Nah, I'm good at hiding. I'll make sure to get as far from here as possible, never to be seen or heard. Don't ya worry 'bout me, I'll be fine!

- Thank you, Rodrick, I mean it!

- Don't thank me just yet. Do that once you're outside in safety.

[18] Like an animal.

In the midst of all this arguing, I notice how Estamond is no longer on the sacrifice table, so too, Rodrick is nowhere to be seen. That sneaky bastard, he must've helped Estamond and is now off to running and hiding with her. I'm not going to leave it like this. That knife there, that should be just perfect.

- Where do you think you're going, Galen?

- Sorry Alder but no one is going to keep me from being with my dear Estamond. So do please get out of my way… I won't ask again. You too, Gaius.

- No can do. You are both going to die tonight. Ramon will get back both of them and then we'll kill you both.

- I didn't want to do this but you leave me no choice…

- Ahhh… I can't… I can't feel anything…

- Alder, nooo… Galen you bastard.

- Sorry, Gaius but I did warn you.

- You… you will… pay for this. Mark… my… words.

I didn't want to kill them but they left me no choice. Now… where is Ramon off to? I should hurry and catch him before he gets to Estamond. Now Rodrick, he better not get any funny ideas or he'll meet an unfortunate end too. First is going to be his father though. It'll be payback for hunting me down and getting me trapped in those caves… even though it wasn't really their fault, it was because of them that I ended up in the cave tunnels. Ooh, that's him there.

- I guess old age is finally catching up to you, Ramon?

- Galen… whose is that blood? Don't tell me you killed them both?

- It was coming to them… for all that they did… to those kids… to their families. You have a son, you of all people should understand their pain and suffering.

- I get that… but please, put the knife down… no one else needs to die.

- It all depends on you and your boy, on your next move and his next move. I don't want to do this but I do have to say, I won't feel sorry or any regret in any case.

- Then I'm afraid you've become a murderer just like I had all those years back. Those kids aren't the only people I've killed… there are many more and with each person, it weighed down on me.

- At any given time you could've stopped. And the worst part is, you got your son involved in the murders too… your own son Ramon.

- I now regret every moment, every second of it all.

- Don't you think it's a little too late for that now. And you are only saying all of this because you don't want to die.

- I'm sorry for all the wrong that I have ever done… I truly am. I have sinned long enough so please, do whatever you want with me but spare my son, leave him out of this.

- That's for me to decide and in order to make sure that none of what has happened here happens ever again, I will spare you the sorrow and the pain and set you both free from this world.

- Noo… please no…

Oh my… what… what have I done? Was that really me that did all this? So much blood… everywhere. He was right, I have become one of them… a monster. No, I can't let thoughts like that play tricks on my mind. I have to find my dear Estamond and save her from Rodrick… who knows what he'll do to her. Ah… my hip. Looks like Ramon got me… I can't pass out now, not here. Estamond… got… to get… to my Estamond.

Is that them? Can't see that well now… gets more blurry by the minute.

- Estamond? My love, is that you?

- Galen? Ahh… what happened to you? You're bleeding…

- I'm fine, really. You better get away from him… from Rodrick.

- What? Why? What are you talking about? He saved my life, he freed me and made sure I got to safety.

- That's true Mr Galen. I only wanted lady Estamond to be safe and out of all that trouble.

- My dear Estamond… you cannot trust him. He's not who he makes you think he is. Get away from him… Now!!!

- It's ok Rodrick, you can let me go. I'll be safe. I'll talk to Galen and sort this all out… fidati di me… umm trust me.

- Ok Ms Estamond, I do trust you.

- Galen, my dear… put the knife away. He got me here, you got here, it's all over now. Let him go. He won't harm you and he certainly won't harm me.

- No… he is just like his father and all the rest of them. Fortunately, they won't bother us anymore now.

- What have you done to them? My dear, answer me!!!

- I killed them all… every single one of them. It was them or us, my beloved. I couldn't let them harm you. The only one left is him, that bastard that "saved" you.

- You… you killed my father… papa, I should've been there for you, protecting you, papa…

- I don't believe this… how could you? You are not the Galen I fell in love with… not anymore.

- Rodrick… get away from her… you don't want to… meet the same fate that your father met.

- Just kill me already… there's no point for me to stay on this… this motherland. Papa is dead… kill me too then… just make it quick…

- Now… that makes it five and no more of such people coming after us… it's all over… Rodrick was the last one.

- Oh my… what has happened to you? All these people… dead. How could you? I know you love me but this… this can't be done out of love.

- I can't explain it… nothing I'll say will ever change the fact that I did it or that it'll bring these people back. All I was doing was saving you…

- And I'm thankful for that, you know it, but I didn't want to be saved at the expense of all those lives. My life isn't worth five people's lives no matter how bad they were while alive or because of what they did to us.

- You saw me when I had just walked in. I could see it in your eyes when you looked at me, as if something had changed about me. I know that something has… I can feel it.

- Yes, the Galen that I remember… that I grew to love with all my heart… he wouldn't have done

this. He would've saved me and all these other people.
-All I cared about was saving you, not them… the things I've been through… the things that I've seen… these people didn't deserve to be spared.

- I can't do this anymore… not the way you are now… *Io non ho la forza.*[19]..

- What you mean by "you don't have the strength?"
You can't leave all that we have, you can't give up… I don't want you to.

- It's not about what you want for me, what you think is best for me. It's about dealing with our choices and decisions that we make and I can't do it anymore knowing what you've done… and living with fear that someday, after a year, maybe ten, maybe thirty years, you could do this again… I simply can't do it, I won't do it.

- I don't have the strength to live without you. I can't imagine my life, living like that.
But like you said, it's about what you want, the decisions you make. And I have to respect that… I will respect that.

[19] I don't have the strength.

- Maybe someday somewhere we'll meet again but for a time, maybe infinite, I want to be on my own, think things through. I need to go away and start over…

- So, this is goodbye then… I never had the thought… never even expected we would go our separate ways.

I will miss her, very much so. I do love her and it was her wish to part ways and so, I must respect it. I'll go back to London, get away from this place… it's only led to misfortune and me doing the unthinkable. I'm not going to work either, my mind isn't up for it after all this. I have to carry on living though, no matter how tough it'll get but I will fight.

- Till I see you again my love… Least maybe one last hug then, to soften the pain?

- Yeah, that we can do, I'd like that.
Goodbye then… we might see each other again, who knows.

We did spend, what feels like *un eternità*[20] together, I can't help but to feel sorry for Galen. After all that has happened over the past couple of weeks, what had happened just before we went our

[20] Eternity.

separate ways, I can't just that easily go back to the way things were before. My mind wouldn't let me… I wouldn't let myself carry on. It's just me now and my own journey.

- I do feel we will meet again but until then, I wish you all the best my dear Galen, *Arrivederci amore mio*[21]…

[21] Goodbye my love.

-*Mr* Olmstead, how are you feeling today?

- Who? What? What has happened? Who's Mr Olmstead? That's not my name!

- So, you haven't started to remember anything then…

- Remember what? I don't even know who you are and why I'm here!

- Well, according to these files, your name is Mr Joshua Simmons. Born in 1987, place of birth unknown.

- No, that's not my name. My name is Galen Mitchell and I was born in the 19th century, 1840 to be exact in West Midlands. I'm an investigator from London.

- No, Mr Joshua. You're a patient in Owl's Hall Mental Institute… have been for the past three years now. And we have this exact conversation every three months. I'm your doctor, Dr Estamond De Luca. You have a condition - personality disorder. You have killed people as a result of your disorder, five people to be exact.

- Can't be… how could this be real? This must be a nightmare. I don't believe you, not even for one second. This is just too unreal to be true. All that I've seen and experienced, that was real, not this crap you are telling me. I do know I've killed people but that was in order to save her…

- To be honest, I'm getting tired of this Joshua. I keep hoping that you would snap out of your disorder and just get better, for your own self good. You keep on going back to your 'reality', then waking up here and in the morning your back to your 'reality' again, your there for three months and then once you 'come back' we have this conversation.

- No matter what you say, I still don't believe you! It simply cannot be true…
-Then let me show you. Let's go outside. Outside of this room and maybe then you'll start to believe me.

- Okay, fine, though I still doubt it'll prove me wrong.

- Joshua, please take that newspaper there on the chair and tell me the date on it?

- It says "Wednesday, 3rd of June, 2019"…

- So, you still don't believe me?

- Slowly but yeah, I might be starting to believe you. It's just all so much to take in all at once.

- I understand that, it's only normal you'd find it hard to believe. It's just that we've done this so many times now… well apart from you leaving your room, this is a first.

- Can I ask you a question?

- Sure, ask away…

- Is my disorder treatable, fully I mean, so it doesn't return? Like in a way that I either 'stay' here or go back there and never wake up again?

- Well, so far, the methods and the treatment that we've tried, none of it has worked… not yet anyways. We'll keep on trying but there are no guarantees. I need you to collaborate as well, to try harder to snap out of it, to accept the reality, to face the reality for what it is.

- You know, I killed those people. I have to live with that. That's why I created the other reality in my mind, it's easier that way, in my mind I mean… till I kill those people, after that it's hard to cope again. Shortly after, I wake up in this apparent reality.

- There isn't anything else that we can do, none of the methods has worked. I guess that not until you can face what you've done and accept it, however tough of a decision it may be, we are just going to keep on coming back to this situation. Nonetheless, I'm not giving up on you…

- Okay doctor… I'll try. I can't promise anything though.

- I'll be happy even if you tried your best but didn't succeed. So, I'll see you tomorrow then Joshua.

- Goodnight doctor.

What Dr Estamond told me yesterday… I still find it hard to believe. I know I got to see things, to go outside and to see it all for my own eyes. I know in the back of my mind that I made up another reality… makes it easier that way, otherwise, I would find it very hard to live.

It's been so long now, I don't think that I even remember anymore why it was that I killed those people. I know that I was a good person, had a loving and caring family, a good job and then one day, step by step, it all went overly wrong. Next thing I knew, I had lost everything and the only thing that was on my mind was getting revenge on the people that had destroyed my life. To make sure that they know how I felt like, in all that rage, I had killed them all. Do I regret my actions? Something's telling me that I do not and that I shouldn't regret any of it. However, I was unable to cope with it. That's why I spent all this time in the safe heaven that I had created, my nineteenth century. A place where it's all different, the world is different, I'm different… was different. I still have unfinished business there.

I'm not fully sure, but I believe I overheard the doctors say that they want to euthanize me. The treatment has been "unsuccessful" and so, I can't be cured. Of course, in order for them to euthanize me, they need my consent, my signed consent. Well, guess what? They ain't getting it. I rather live like this than become an empty, selfless shell that is, just an empty nothingness. No way, I'm just not going to let them do that. I'll escape tonight, after lights out. Go into hiding and travel the world. Maybe go to Egypt perhaps… India is nice as well and most definitely Italy.

I've realised that I can't go on like this any longer… not in here anyways, maybe even not in this time. I heard what the doctors were saying and how they want to euthanize me, but that's not what I want. I want to live, to go on adventures… real adventures this time. You were right in saying that I need to face the consequences of my actions.

And I will do it, just in my own way and definitely not in here… somewhere far away from here, in peace and quiet, free from all the worries. There's also nothing that's keeping me here… my family is long gone now, as I'm sure you know that. So why would I stay here? You know the treatment hasn't worked but no one has tried, whenever I've come back, to let me go out on my own, far away from everything. Maybe… just maybe, this is the one thing that can help me, simply forgetting about everything? 'Locking' out of everything? Maybe… medication is the one thing that just isn't going to work in my case? Now, this doesn't mean that you're a bad doctor all of a sudden. No, not at all. This just means that this time it might be the simplest thing, that you can possibly think of, that is going to save me. This is the 'sane' me talking here, and I don't know for how long that's going to last, so I'm asking of you only one thing… while I still can… please, just let me escape tonight, no guards to be following me, none. I'll be on my way and out of your picture.

I don't want to be put into eternal sleep while I still have unfinished business. This is my only wish that I ask of you, not to go after me and simply let me be. You'll hear from me or about me, one way or another, whether it be good or bad or nothing at all. That's when you'll know your next step to take… big or small will be up to you to decide.

This is me saying 'goodbye' and farewell to the one person that hasn't given up on me… and may we see each other again, whether in this lifetime or another is not for us to decide.

~~Gal~~ Joshua.

About the Author

Well, I'm twenty-two years old and originally from Latvia and have been living in Ireland for the past seven years. Did my secondary school here, three years of college, which I do not consider a waste, worked and now here we are.

Writing… it was something that I've been good at but never thought of it as a hobby, let alone to write a book. What started as a twenty-page story is now a published book.

I'm not big into talking about myself like this, so I won't waste any more of your time. Go on now and turn to page one to enter *A Midsummer's Enigma…*

Printed in Poland
by Amazon Fulfillment
Poland Sp. z o.o., Wrocław

58332678R00061